The Rain Forest

Animals of the Rain Forest

Mae Woods

ABDO Publishing Company

visit us at
www.abdopub.com

Published by Abdo Publishing Company 4940 Viking Drive, Edina, Minnesota 55435.
Copyright © 1999 by Abdo Consulting Group, Inc. International copyrights reserved in all
countries. No part of this book may be reproduced in any form without written permission
from the publisher.

Printed in the United States.

Photo credits: Peter Arnold, Inc.

Edited by Lori Kinstad Pupeza
Contributing editor Morgan Hughes
Graphics by Linda O'Leary

Library of Congress Cataloging-in-Publication Data

Woods, Mae.
      Animals of the rain forest / Mae Woods.
      p. cm. -- (The rain forest)
      Includes index.
      Summary: Examines the physical characteristics and behaviors of
      various animals found in the rain forest, including monkeys, jungle
      cats, and frogs.
      ISBN 1-57765-019-0
      1. Rain forest animals--Juvenile literature. [1. Rain forest animals.] I. Title. II.
      Series: Woods, Mae. Rain forest.
      QL112.W66 1999
      591.734--dc21   98-9814
                                      CIP
                                      AC

Note to reader
The words in the text that are the color green refer to the words in the glossary.

Contents

Animals of the Rain Forest

*T*he rain forest provides a wonderful habitat, or home, for an animal. Just as the plants in a rain forest live in different layers, so do the animals. In the dim understory and forest floor are the larger creatures: elephants, gorillas, deer, wild pigs, and jungle cats.

The canopy level has the most plant life and attracts the most animals. There, trees are filled with the sounds of birds and monkeys. Frogs, snakes, lizards, squirrels, rats, and mice also live in canopy trees.

This illustration shows the different layers in a rain forest.

Emergents

Canopy

Understory

Forest Floor

Many fascinating and strange animals live in rain forests. People still discover new species there. For years, beautiful animals have disappeared because they have been hunted for their skins or sold as pets. Animals also disappear if their habitats change. When trees are cut down, there is less food. Animals move to new areas or die. As a result, there are now many endangered species in rain forests.

A tapir of the Amazon rain forest.

Monkeys

Monkeys live in all levels of rain forests. Some species eat fruit, some eat leaves. Different groups are able to live side by side in peace because they do not fight for food.

In South America, monkeys have bare faces and tails that can grasp tree trunks or food. Some are very small. The pygmy marmoset is the size of a mouse. The muriqui is the largest monkey in this region, and sadly the most endangered. Only a few hundred live in the wild. The capuchin is the most common species along with the howler monkey, named for its loud voice. The spider monkey has woolly fur and a long tail that it uses like an extra hand. A bright mane of hair sticks out around the golden lion tamarin's face. It is now very rare.

Different species of monkeys live in Africa and Asia. The mandrill has a brightly colored face and stumpy tail. The colobus monkey, known for its climbing skill, has a straight tail.

A golden lion tamarin in the Amazon rain forest.

Apes

Apes, such as gorillas, gibbons, chimpanzees, and orangutans, are found in the rain forests of Africa and Asia. Apes have no tails and are larger and more intelligent than monkeys.

Chimpanzees are at home on the ground or in the trees. They sleep in the trees where they build fresh nests of leaves and branches each night. They spend the day searching for fruit and leaves to eat. Of all animals, chimpanzees are most like humans. Scientists discovered that chimpanzees are even smart enough to learn sign language.

Like chimps, orangutans have long, muscular arms and can use their flexible toes like fingers. They have long orange hair. Orangutans are found in Borneo and Sumatra. The gibbon is the smallest ape and the best climber. The gorilla is too big to climb trees.

A gibbon
hanging from a
tree in Thailand.

9

Jungle Cats

*T*igers, jaguars, leopards, and ocelots are jungle cats. All are excellent hunters. They see and hear better than humans. Pads on their feet allow them to move quietly. They have strong, sharp claws for climbing trees and attacking their prey. Cats like to hunt at night when their colored coats blend in with the plants. They are meat eaters. All animals fear them. Jungle cats eat wild pig, deer, sloths, and monkeys. They will even attack elephants and people.

The tiger, a striped cat, lives in the jungles of Southeast Asia and India. The spotted jaguar lives in Central and South America. The smaller ocelot also lives in Central and South America. Its unique coat has both stripes and spots.

In Africa, the yellow and brown spotted leopard is the best hunter in the rain forest. The fierce panther is actually a kind of leopard. It has black spots on black fur, so it looks one color.

A Bengal tiger.

Birds

*O*ne out of three bird species in the world live in rain forests. Tropical birds feed on fruit and insects, which are always plentiful. The toucan, macaw, bird of paradise, parakeet, parrot, and cockatoo are known for their vivid colors and unique calls. The toucan and macaw have unusual-looking beaks used to pick fruit or to crack nuts.

One special kind of bird, the quetzal, has a bright red chest and long, green tail feathers. It eats small avocado-like fruits. It digests the soft pulp then coughs up the seed.

There are three species of tropical eagles: the monkey-eating eagle in the Philippines, the crowned eagle in Africa, and the harpy eagle in South America. The harpy eagle is the largest and most powerful bird. It flies 50 miles per hour (80 kmph) and is a fierce hunter with claws as large as a man's hand. Not many fly through the forests anymore.

The colorful quetzal
of the Costa Rican
rain forest.

Bats

Many different kinds of bats live in rain forests. Some are named for the food they hunt. There are bird-eating, lizard-eating, frog-eating, and blood-eating bats.

The most **common** species are fruit bats. They eat fruit and insects. Most bats are blind. They are guided by sound waves when they fly. They sleep in the tree tops all day and come out at night to feed.

There are special bats in Africa and Asia that hunt by day and can see. They are larger than other kinds of bats. The biggest, the Malaysian flying fox, has a wingspan of six feet (two m). The vampire bat is small, but it has sharp, curved front teeth.

Bats play important roles in rain forest life. Bat droppings contain seeds from the fruit they eat. These seeds scatter on the forest floors. The seeds will sprout into new plants for the animals to eat.

A fruit bat feeding.

Snakes

*T*he largest kind of snake is the python, and it lives in the rain forest. One species in Indonesia is over 30 feet long (9 m). It wraps its long body around its **prey** and squeezes it to death. Pythons have been known to eat humans. They usually hunt monkeys, birds, and wild pigs. The fer-de-lance is the most dangerous snake in the jungle. Its powerful **venom** can kill within seconds.

Many snakes have skins that blend in with the plants and trees where they live. This makes it easy for them to sneak up on their prey. The green tree python looks like a branch of a tree. It feeds on birds, tree frogs, and other small animals.

Snakes that are poisonous often have bright markings. Coral snakes have red, yellow, and black bands around their bodies. Once animals learn which snakes are dangerous, they can easily spot them and run away.

16

The poisonous coral snake.

Frogs and Lizards

The trees in the rain forests are home to some unique frogs and lizards—they can fly! Flying frogs have large, webbed toes. These open like tiny parachutes when they jump into the air. Flying lizards have flaps of skin on the sides of their bodies that work like wings.

A tree frog will lay its eggs on the leaves of a bromeliad, a plant shaped like the top of a pineapple. Pools of rain collect in the cones at the base of the plant. Here, the eggs hatch into tadpoles, which stay in the water until they grow into frogs. Salamanders, snails, and beetles also live in these tiny ponds.

One species of frog called the poison dart frog makes a deadly poison. The poison dart frog has light and dark blue markings all over its body. Hunters remove poison from the frog and put it on the tips of their arrows and darts.

A poison dart frog.

Water Animals

Very unusual animals live in the rivers and along their banks. Some are fierce. Crocodiles such as the black caiman thrive in the Amazon River. The giant anaconda snake grows to nearly 40 feet (12 m) long. It feeds on caiman, fish, and animals on the river banks. Pink dolphins also live in the rivers. They help protect smaller animals by eating savage piranha fish.

The manatee, sometimes called a sea cow, has flippers and a broad, flat tail. It eats water plants. Electric eels, found in the Amazon River, carry shocks up to 650 volts, enough to stun a horse.

The capybara, the world's largest rodent, lives on the river bank where it can find a kind of grass it likes to eat. It is four feet (one m) long. The skin between its toes allows it to swim. The tapir has hoofed feet and a snout like a short trunk. It swims and eats plants.

The capybara, the world's largest rodent.

Glossary

Canopy (KAN-o-pee) - the middle, upper level of the rain forest that is thick with vines and trees.

Common - often seen or heard; widespread.

Endangered species - a group of animals in danger of becoming extinct.

Fascinating - interesting.

Grasp - to grip or hold on to something.

Habitat (HAB-uh-tat) - the place where a plant or animal lives; its natural surroundings.

Plentiful (PLEN-tee-full) - in great supply; more than enough.

Prey - an animal that is caught to be eaten.

Sign language - a way of talking with hand signals. Sign language is used mainly by people who are deaf.

Skill - special ability; excellence.

Understory - the middle, lower level of the rain forest between the ground and the canopy.

Venom (VEN-ahm) - the poison of a snake or spider.

Internet Sites

Amazon Interactive
http://www.eduweb.com/amazon.html
Explore the geography of the Ecuadorian rain forest through on-line games and
activities. Discover the ways that the Quichua live off the land.

Living Edens: Manu, Peru's Hidden Rain Forest
http://www.pbs.org/edens/manu/
This site is about the animals and indigenous people who populate Peru's Manu
region.

The Rain Forest Workshop
http://kids.osd.wednet.edu/Marshall/rainforest_home_page.html
The Rain Forest Workshop was developed by Virginia Reid and the students at
Thurgood Marshall Middle School, in Olympia, Washington. This site is one of the
best school sites around with links to many other sites as well as great information on
the rain forest.

The Tropical Rain Forest in Suriname
http://www.euronet.nl/users/mbleeker/suriname/suri-eng.html
A multimedia tour through the rain forest in Suriname (SA). Read about plants,
animals, Indians and Maroons. This site is very organized and full of information.

These sites are subject to change. Go to your favorite search engine and type in
Rain Forest for more sites.

Pass It On

Rain Forest Enthusiasts: educate readers around the country by passing
on information you've learned about rain forests. Share your little-known
facts and interesting stories. Tell others about animals, insects, or people of
the rain forest. We want to hear from you!
To get posted on the ABDO Publishing Company website E-mail us at
"Science@abdopub.com"
Visit the ABDO Publishing Company website at www.abdopub.com

Index